SATURN

GOD OF SOWING OF SEEDS

by Teri Temple and Emily Temple
Illustrated by Eric Young

The Child's World

Published by The Child's World®
1980 Lookout Drive • Mankato, MN 56003-1705
800-599-READ • www.childsworld.com

ACKNOWLEDGMENTS
The Child's World®: Mary Berendes, Publishing Director
Red Line Editorial: Editorial direction
The Design Lab: Design and production
Design elements ©: Banana Republic Images/Shutterstock Images; Shutterstock Images; Anton Balazh/Shutterstock Images
Photographs ©: Viacheslav Lopatin/Shutterstock Images, 5; Eyüp Alp Ermis/Shutterstock Images, 10; Styve Reineck/Shutterstock Images, 12; Matham, 16; akg-images/Newscom, 20; Public Domain, 23; Shutterstock Images, 24; Jaan-Martin Kuusmann/Shutterstock Images, 29

ISBN 9781631437243
LCCN 2014945312

Printed in the United States of America
Mankato, MN
November, 2014
PA02241

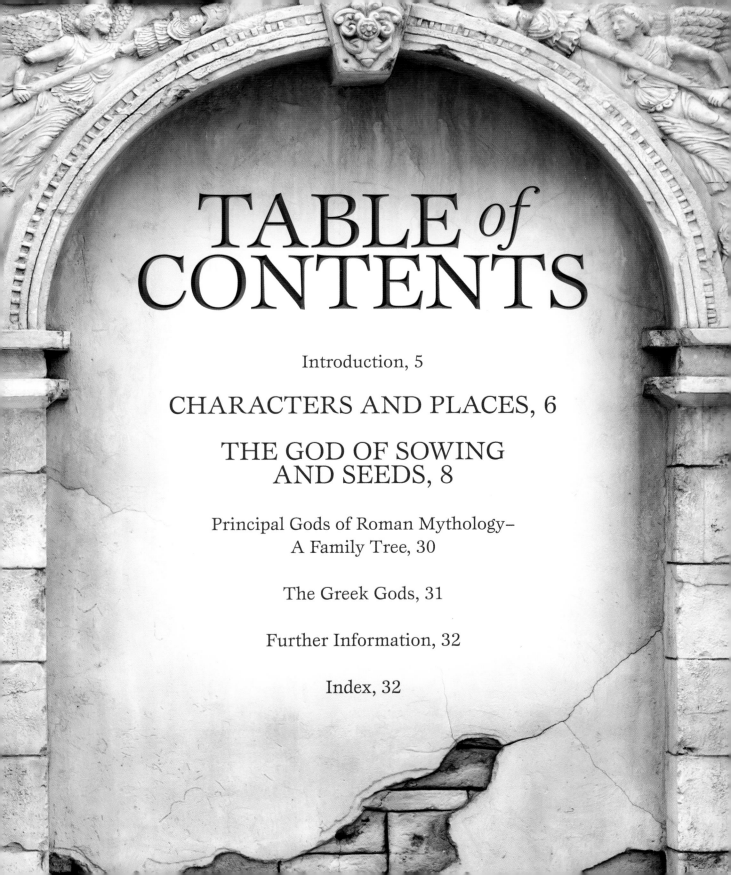

TABLE *of* CONTENTS

INTRODUCTION

In ancient times Romans believed in spirits or gods called numina. In Latin, *numina* means divine will or power. The Romans took part in religious rituals to please the gods. They felt the gods had powers that could make their lives better.

As the Roman government grew more powerful, its armies conquered many neighboring lands. Romans often adopted beliefs from these new cultures. They greatly admired the Greek arts and sciences. Gradually, the Romans combined the Greek myths and religion with their own. These stories shaped and influenced each part of a Roman citizen's daily life. Ancient Roman poets, such as Ovid and Virgil, wrote down these tales of wonder. Their writings became a part of Rome's great history. To the Romans, however, these stories were not just for entertainment. Roman mythology was their key to understanding the world.

ANCIENT ROMAN SOCIETIES
Ancient Roman society was divided into several groups. The patricians were the most powerful and wealthiest group. They often owned land and held power in the government. The plebeians worked for the patricians. Slaves were prisoners of war or children without parents. Some slaves were freed and enjoyed most of the rights of citizens.

CHARACTERS AND PLACES

ANCIENT ROME

ADRIATIC SEA

ROME

TYRRHENIAN SEA

N
W E
S

CAELUS *(CEE-lus)*

The sky and heavens; born of Terra along with the mountains and seas; husband of Terra; father of the Titans, Cyclopes, and Hecatoncheires

CYCLOPES *(SIGH-clopes)*

One-eyed giants; children of Terra and Caelus

HECATONCHEIRES *(hek-a-TON-kear-eez)*

Monstrous creatures with 100 arms and 50 heads; children of Terra and Caelus

JUPITER *(JOO-pi-ter)*

Supreme ruler of the heavens and of the gods who lived on Mount Olympus; son of Saturn and Ops; married to Juno; father of many gods and heroes

NEPTUNE *(NEP-toon)*

God of the seas and storms; brother to Jupiter

OPS *(ops)*

A Titaness; married to her brother Saturn; mother to the first six Olympic gods: Jupiter, Neptune, Pluto, Juno, Vesta & Ceres

PLUTO *(PLOO-toh)*

God of the underworld and death; son of Saturn and Ops, married to Proserpine

SATURN *(SAT-ern)*

A Titan who ruled the world; married to Ops and their children became the first six Olympic gods

TERRA *(TER-uh)*

Mother Earth and one of the first elements born to Chaos; mother of the Titans, Cyclopes, and Hecatoncheires

VENUS *(VEE-nuhs)*

Goddess of love and beauty; born of the sea foam; wife of Vulcan; mother of Cupid

CHAOS: *The formless darkness that existed at the beginning of time*

TITANS: *The 12 children of Terra and Caelus; godlike giants who are said to represent the forces of nature*

THE GOD OF
SOWING AND SEEDS

The god Saturn is one of the oldest figures in ancient Roman tradition. He was known as a caretaker god. It was Saturn's job to protect the harvest. He did so with his wife, Ops. The Romans would have a feast each year to thank Saturn for watching their crops.

The Greek god Cronus was often confused with the god of time, Chronus. This caused Saturn's appearance to also change. Romans began to view him as elderly. Saturn had white hair and a beard. This matched the god of time.

Through all of the changes, Saturn's purpose remained the same. His Latin name, *Saturnus*, means the god of sowing and seeds. Though he was connected to Cronus, Saturn was most similar to the Greek goddess Demeter. She represented grains, summertime, and the harvest.

The Roman tradition may have changed Saturn's image over time, but the story of his birth remained the same.

Long before humans were created, there was nothing. Ancient Romans called this nothingness Chaos. Mother Earth rose out of Chaos to create the universe. Mother Earth was also given the name Terra.

Terra gave birth to Caelus, or Father Sky. Caelus represented the heavens and the sky. He became Terra's husband. They ruled over creation together.

Terra and Caelus had many children. Their children included three Cyclopes, three Hecatoncheires, and seven mighty Titans. The Cyclopes were giant creatures with one eye in the middle of their foreheads. Cyclopes were skilled builders and craftsmen. Hecatoncheires were monsters with 150 hands and 50 heads. They were fearsome beasts and violent warriors.

LATIN VERSUS GREEK
In ancient times, people spoke the language of the district where they lived. The Romans lived in the district of Latium in Italy. Their language became known as Latin. When the Romans combined the Greek myths and stories with their own, they changed the names of some of the gods. In Latin, Mother Earth became Terra. Uranus was called Caelus.

The Titans were the most marvelous of Terra
and Caelus's children. Titans had remarkable
strength. They represented the forces of
nature. One of these Titans was the
mighty Saturn.

Caelus thought his monstrous children were ugly. Their appearance disgusted him. He was also afraid of the Titans' great power. He decided to hide all of his children in the center of the earth.

Terra was very unhappy. Caelus had locked her children away in the underworld. Terra thought this was cruel. She did not agree with his treatment of their children. She wanted to free them, but she needed help. She asked her children to help her defeat Caelus. Only Saturn agreed.

ROMAN MONSTERS
When the ancient Romans discovered great bones buried in the earth, they made up stories about them. They believed the first creatures to walk the earth were the Cyclopes, the Hecatoncheires, and the Giants. The children of Terra and Caelus were not like humans. They were monsters. They had strength and powers. They believed the bones came from these great monsters. Archeologists have since proved these bones actually belonged to dinosaurs.

Terra gave Saturn a special, unbreakable weapon. Saturn took the weapon and waited for his father. When Caelus arrived, Saturn used his powerful weapon to defeat his father. Saturn freed his siblings and spilled his father's blood into the ocean. Caelus's remains mixed with the

ocean foam. The goddess Venus was formed. His blood also
formed the Giants and the Erinyes. The Erinyes had snakes
for hair and blood for tears. They punished evildoers. Now
Saturn and his siblings would rule the earth.

After defeating his father, Saturn became king of the Titans. The Titans were considered the elder gods of the Roman religion. Though Saturn was the most famous, each Titan was recognized in his or her own right.

Saturn's brother Oceanus also married a sister, Tethys. Oceanus guarded the river that surrounded the earth. Tethys was the goddess of freshwater.

Saturn's siblings Coeus and Phoebe married as well. Coeus and Phoebe eventually became grandparents to the Olympic gods, Apollo and Diana.

Saturn's brother Hyperion was the guardian of light. Moneta and Themis were two of Saturn's sisters. Moneta, also known as Mnemosyne, was the goddess of memory. It was believed she created language. Themis was a counselor.

The Titans lived in Olympus. It was a great palace at the top of the highest mountain in Thessaly, Greece. Olympus was hidden from humans by a gate of clouds. The weather was perfect inside Olympus. The Titans dined on ambrosia and nectar, special foods that allowed them to live forever.

Saturn and Ops became the king and queen of the Titans. The Titans ruled the universe. Ops represented wealth and resources. She was Saturn's helper in the harvest. Eventually Saturn and Ops had children of their own. This made Saturn nervous.

Saturn had defeated his father, Caelus, years earlier. As a result, Saturn thought it was his destiny to be overthrown by one of his own children. When Ops began having children, he came up with a plan to prevent his downfall.

When each child was born, Saturn would immediately swallow it. Having them in his stomach meant they could not cause him harm. However, this made Ops sad. Ops had a plan when their sixth child, Jupiter, was born.

SATURN AND LUA MATER

In earlier times, Saturn was associated with another female goddess. Her name was Lua Mater. Not much is known about Lua Mater. Some historians think she may have been a version of Ops that changed as stories were shared. She was a mysterious earth goddess. Her name was connected with destruction and plague. Sometimes armies took the weapons of an enemy they had defeated and burned them as a sacrifice to her. They hoped this would help them avoid punishment.

Ops went to the Island of Crete to give birth to Jupiter. She left Jupiter on the island and returned to Saturn with a stone wrapped in clothes. Saturn thought the heavy stone was Jupiter and swallowed it. Saturn thought he was safe, but Ops had tricked him and saved one of their children.

A woodland nymph raised Jupiter. Saturn thought he had swallowed Jupiter and was saved from being overthrown. He was wrong. When Jupiter grew into a man, he returned and forced his father to face his destiny.

Jupiter and Terra forced Saturn to throw up all of his children. The five children of Ops and Saturn were free. They became the first Olympic gods.

The gods were angry with Saturn for imprisoning them for so long. They started a war against their father. Jupiter and his brothers talked with their uncles, the Cyclopes and the Hecatoncheires. The fearsome Hecatoncheires agreed to fight with the gods against their brother, Saturn. The Cyclopes made them special weapons. They gave Jupiter lightning and thunderbolts.

The war lasted ten years. It was so fierce, the universe nearly collapsed. With the Hecatoncheires and the Cyclopes' weapons on their side, Jupiter and the gods defeated their father.

Jupiter had fulfilled the prophecy. Saturn's own children overthrew him. The Olympic gods would now rule the universe.

According to myth, there are two stories of the war. In both versions the gods are victors. How they achieve victory changes in each story.

In the first story, after Jupiter defeated his father, he imprisoned Saturn and the Titans in the underworld. The Titans were to remain there for eternity.

With the Titans imprisoned, Jupiter and his siblings assumed their position as the rulers of the universe. Jupiter's siblings were Neptune, Pluto, Ceres, Vesta, and Juno. They were the first six Olympic gods.

Jupiter became the king of the gods. He gave each of his brothers reign over a separate part of the universe. Jupiter went on to have children with his sister, Juno. Their children brought the number of Olympic gods to 12.

UNDERWORLD
Ancient Roman philosophers believed the earth was a flat disc. The disc was divided into two equal parts by a sea. Today we call that sea the Mediterranean. A river surrounded the disc. The dome of heaven covered it. Deep beneath the earth was the underworld. It is where the gods locked up their enemies. Ancient Romans believed the gods lived in the heavens, humans walked on the earth, and the Titans were imprisoned in the underworld.

The Olympic gods brought with them an age of peace. They took their thrones on Mount Olympus. From their new home, they ruled over the world.

Another myth claims that when Saturn was overthrown, Jupiter sent him into exile. Saturn was banished from Mount Olympus for the rest of his life. He eventually found himself in Italy.

Saturn arrived in Italy with nothing. He was stripped of his throne and considered a fugitive. In Italy, he met King Janus. Saturn was the protector of the harvest. He shared his knowledge of agriculture with the people of Italy. He also showed them the workings of civilization. King Janus was pleased with these gifts. As a reward, Saturn was given a share of the kingdom.

Saturn became the king of his new territory. His reign was marked by peace and satisfaction. The humans were well fed from the crops of the earth. They were happy with Saturn as their king.

Saturn was remembered for his generosity. He is often thought of as the father of Rome because of his contributions to the city. Some poets even referred to his time as the Golden Age.

OVID'S FOUR AGES OF MAN

Ovid was a poet who lived in ancient Rome. He is best known for writing a narrative poem called *Metamorphoses*. *Metamorphoses* describes the four ages of man. The first is the Golden Age. This came during the reign of Saturn and was marked by peace. The Silver Age began when Jupiter took over from his father. During the Bronze Age, war was prevalent. The last era was the Iron Age. Still locked in a warlike state, humankind was greedy and stopped worshipping the gods.

During Saturn's Golden Age in Rome, he had a son, Picus. Like his father, Picus would eventually become king in Italy. He became the first king of Latium.

Picus was very handsome. The nymphs and naiads of the forest tried to win his heart. Eventually a beautiful nymph named Canens succeeded and became his wife. Together they had a son named Faunus.

Picus was extremely devoted to his wife. A witch named Circe was jealous that Canens was the object of Picus's affections. One day while Picus was out hunting in the woods, Circe tried to seduce him with charms and potions. Picus rejected her. Circe was so angry that she turned him into a woodpecker.

FAUNUS
Faunus was the son of Picus and Canens. Faunus was identified with the Greek god Pan. Both were represented as being half man and half goat. Faunus was worshiped for making the fields and flocks fruitful. Eventually he became known as a woodland god. He was a prophet who could tell men the meanings of their dreams. He had many festivals. During big celebrations, children would dress as goats and wave goatskins in the air.

Picus's hunting companions found the woodpecker and urged Circe to turn him back. She refused. She turned the companions into beasts and other creatures.

Canens heard of Picus's fate and fled to the woods in search of him. She looked for six days but still could not find her love. Eventually she grew so weary and sad. She lay down on the banks of the Tiber River and died.

In ancient times, Roman myths had great influence on the way people lived. Emperors used the names of gods and goddesses to signify certain times of the year. Saturn's feast day was also one of the most important days in Rome. The timing of Saturn's festival corresponded with the blessing of his temple. It went from December 17 to December 23. During Saturn's festival, Romans celebrated the harvest. It was a time of great feasting.

On Saturn's feast days everyone was equal. Slaves and masters traded places and ate together at the same table. Schools and the government were closed. All business was saved until after the festival. The people of Rome enjoyed the relaxed rules and gave gifts to each other.

Early Christians adopted Saturn's festival and renamed it Christmas. As a result, Christmas is a season marked with eating and gift giving. Though the stories of Saturn come from a long time ago, the Roman myths can tell us a lot about ancient civilizations and the way they influence us today.

Some of the names of gods and goddesses are still being used. Emperor Julius Caesar used the names of Roman gods to create the modern calendar. Saturn even had his own day, Saturday. Stars and planets were also named after gods and goddesses. Mercury, Mars, Venus, Saturn, and Jupiter had planets named after them. Even without a telescope, ancient astronomers could see these planets.

Over time, Saturn's influence on the Roman people faded. However, his temple is one of the few ancient temples still recognized today. Regardless of Saturn's fall from greatness, he, his siblings, and his offspring had great influence on the ancient world.

THE PLANET SATURN

Saturn was one of five planets ancient astronomers could see with the naked eye. It is the second largest planet in our solar system. It was considered the most beautiful object in the universe because of its brilliant rings. Saturn's rings are made up of many moons that encircle the planet. The moons also have the names of characters in Roman mythology, such as Titan, Janus, Pan, and many more.

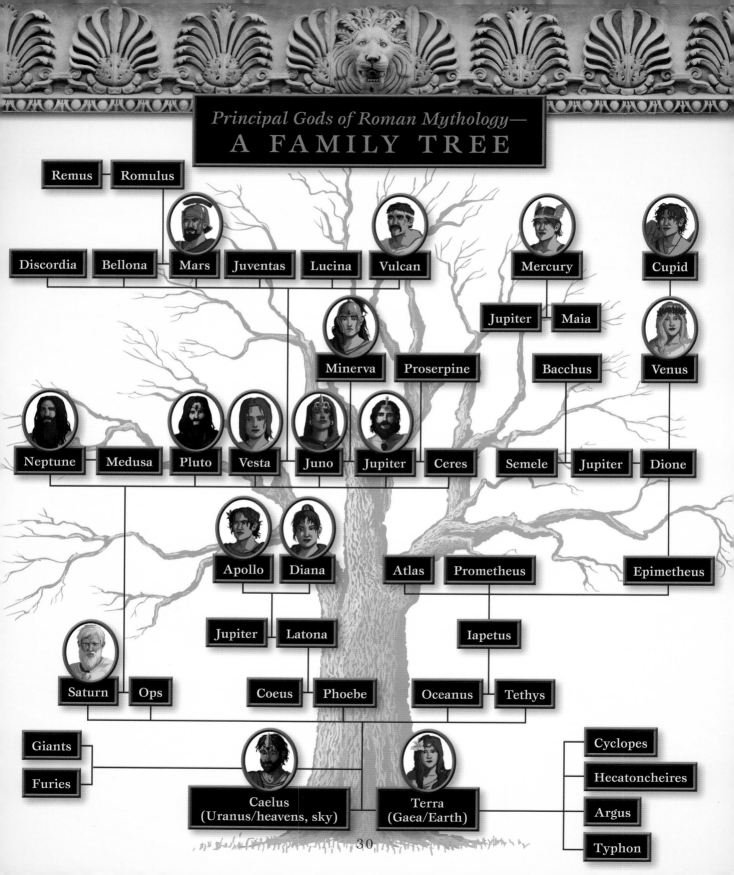

Principal Gods of Roman Mythology—
A FAMILY TREE

Remus — Romulus

Discordia — Bellona — Mars — Juventas — Lucina — Vulcan — Mercury — Cupid

Jupiter — Maia

Minerva — Proserpine — Bacchus — Venus

Neptune — Medusa — Pluto — Vesta — Juno — Jupiter — Ceres — Semele — Jupiter — Dione

Apollo — Diana — Atlas — Prometheus — Epimetheus

Jupiter — Latona — Iapetus

Saturn — Ops — Coeus — Phoebe — Oceanus — Tethys

Giants — Furies — Caelus (Uranus/heavens, sky) — Terra (Gaea/Earth) — Cyclopes — Hecatoncheires — Argus — Typhon

30

THE GREEK GODS

Ancient Greeks believed gods and goddesses ruled the world. The gods fell in love and struggled for power, but they never died. The ancient Greeks believed their gods were immortal. The Greek people worshiped the gods in temples. They felt the gods would protect and guide them. Over time, the Romans and many other cultures adopted the Greek myths as their own. While these other cultures changed the names of the gods, many of the stories remain the same.

SATURN: *Cronus*
God of Time and God of Sowing
Symbol: *Sickle or Scythe*

JUPITER: *Zeus*
King of the Gods, God of Sky, Rain, and Thunder
Symbols: *Thunderbolt, Eagle, and Oak Tree*

JUNO: *Hera*
Queen of the Gods, Goddess of Marriage,
  Pregnancy, and Childbirth
Symbols: *Peacock, Cow, and Diadem*
  (Diamond Crown)

NEPTUNE: *Poseidon*
God of the Sea
Symbols: *Trident, Horse, and Dolphin*

PLUTO: *Hades*
God of the Underworld
Symbols: *Invisibility Helmet and Pomegranate*

MINERVA: *Athena*
Goddess of Wisdom, War, and Arts and Crafts
Symbols: *Owl, Shield, Loom, and Olive Tree*

MARS: *Ares*
God of War
Symbols: *Wild Boar, Vulture, and Dog*

DIANA: *Artemis*
Goddess of the Moon and Hunt
Symbols: *Deer, Moon, and Silver Bow and Arrows*

APOLLO: *Apollo*
God of the Sun, Music, Healing, and Prophecy
Symbols: *Laurel Tree, Lyre, Bow, and Raven*

VENUS: *Aphrodite*
Goddess of Love and Beauty
Symbols: *Dove, Swan, and Rose*

CUPID: *Eros*
God of Love
Symbols: *Bow and Arrows*

MERCURY: *Hermes*
Messenger to the Gods, God of Travelers and Trade
Symbols: *Crane, Caduceus, Winged Sandals,*
  and Helmet

FURTHER INFORMATION

BOOKS

Johnson, Robin. *Understanding Roman Myths*. New York: Crabtree Publishing, 2012.

Temple, Teri. *Zeus: King of the Gods, God of the Sky and Storms*. Mankato, MN: Child's World, 2013.

WEB SITES

Visit our Web site for links about Saturn: *childsworld.com/links*

Note to Parents, Teachers, and Librarians: We routinely verify our Web links to make sure they are safe and active sites. So encourage your readers to check them out!

INDEX